Mrs. Hen's Big Surprise

Margaret K. McElderry Books
An imprint of Simon & Schuster Children's Publishing Division
1230 Avenue of the Americas
New York, NY 10020

Printed in France
2 4 6 8 10 9 7 5 3 1

Library of Congress Card Catalog Number: 99-65042
ISBN 0-689-83403-9

Christel Desmoinaux

Mrs. Hen's Big Surprise

Margaret K. McElderry Books

Mrs. Hen lived in a pretty house in the middle
of a meadow. She was sad, though, because
she didn't have a baby chick to love.

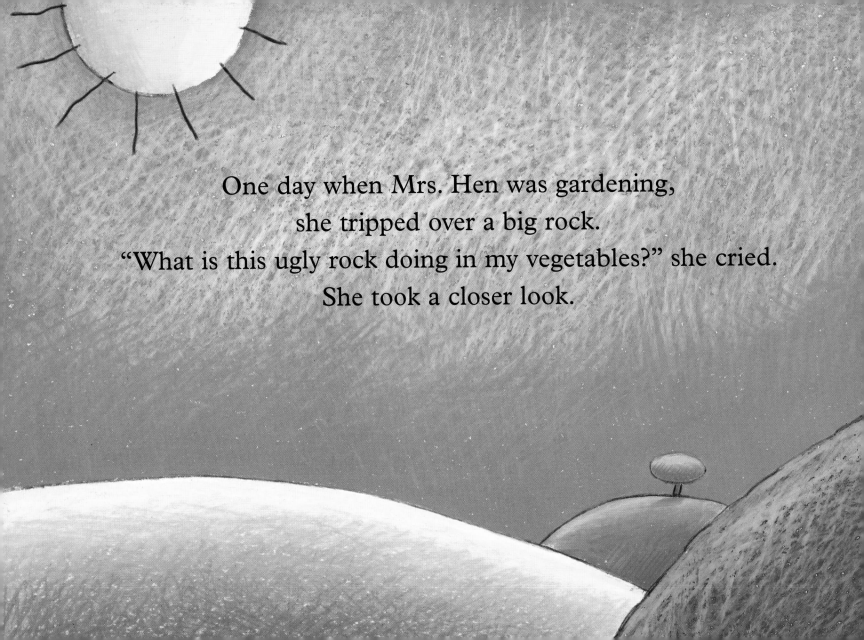

One day when Mrs. Hen was gardening,
she tripped over a big rock.
"What is this ugly rock doing in my vegetables?" she cried.
She took a closer look.

Mrs. Hen dug,
and dug,
and dug,
and dug. . . .

The big rock wasn't a big rock at all.
It was an egg!
Mrs. Hen jumped for joy and shouted,
"I'm going to have a chick! My very own chick!"

Happily, and very carefully, Mrs. Hen wheeled the beautiful egg up the hill. Then she set the egg down in her living room and, like the good hen that she was, she sat on it.

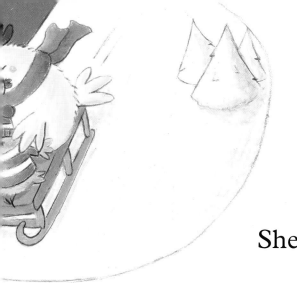

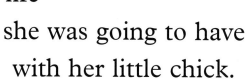

She sat on that egg
and knitted,
imagining the wonderful life
she was going to have
with her little chick.

A few days later, Mrs. Cow came to visit. Mrs. Hen told Mrs. Cow her incredible story.

"Soon I'm going to be the mother of a handsome chick," she said proudly.

Mrs. Cow told the whole story to Mrs. Pig.

"I think our friend Mrs. Hen has some bizarre ideas,"
Mrs. Cow confided. "She's sitting on a very strange-looking
egg she found in her vegetable garden—
and she thinks it's going to hatch into a chick!"

Mrs. Pig told Mrs. Goose . . .

. . . who told Mrs. Sheep . . .

. . . who told Mrs. Turkey . . .

. . . who told Mrs. Porcupine . . .

. . . and Mrs. Hen received a lot more visitors. But her neighbors made fun of her and whispered that the strange-looking egg was never going to hatch.

So Mrs. Hen sat alone with her egg
and waited . . .

. . . waited . . .

. . . and waited some more.
But the seasons passed and
still the egg did not hatch.

Mrs. Hen wanted to help
the egg hatch. She wobbled the egg.
She jostled the egg.
But nothing happened.

"Are you going to hatch or not?"
she cried.

Sadly, Mrs. Hen decided to roll the egg back down to the garden. But suddenly the egg rolled away from Mrs. Hen. Faster and faster it rolled, until it landed with a *CRACK!* at the bottom of the hill.

CRACK! CRACK!
WHAT A SURPRISE!
Two big feet emerged from the broken shell
and the egg started to walk!
Mrs. Hen hurried down the hill as fast
as she could go.

CRACK!
A huge head appeared at
the top of the egg!

"My beloved chick!" cried Mrs. Hen.
"You've finally come!"

For sure, it was a funny-looking chick.
It didn't have feathers or a beak.
And it wasn't yellow. But Mrs. Hen didn't care.
She hugged her chick tight and welcomed him
to the world.

The neighbors were amazed.

It was a happy day for Mrs. Hen.
She and her chick began the life
Mrs. Hen had always dreamed about.

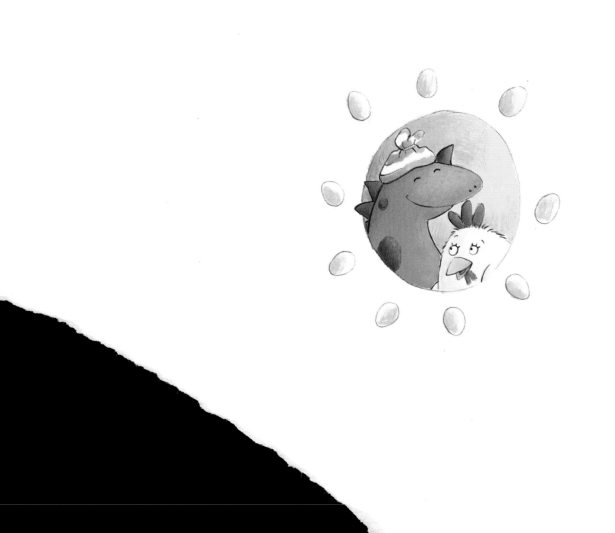